Stalked by the Mafia Prince

EMMA BRAY

Blurb

She's his obsession...

Grace Birmingham is my obsession. One look is all it takes to embed her into my soul. She's a bright ray of light shining in my dark world, and I want her.

I want her more than I've ever wanted anything in my life.

As the mafia prince, I'm not used to denying myself anything, but my little Gracie has secrets even she doesn't know about—secrets that could bring my entire empire crashing down.

I know what I should do, but I'll burn this city to the ground before I let anything happen to *mi tesoro, mi princesa.*

No matter what happens, Grace Birmingham is *mine.*

Chapter One

Massimo

"I DON'T CARE what you have to do. Just get it done." I hang up the phone and check my Rolex, irritated when I note that Rocco is late once again. I'm really getting tired of dealing with him, but until my father dies and leaves me in charge, I'm stuck taking orders. Unfortunately, it comes with the job description I was handed the day I was born. Still, I don't have to put up with this kind of disrespect.

I drum my fingers against the door of the limo as I lift my glass of Sazerac to my lips. My eyes scan the sidewalk through the dark windows, ever vigilant. Men in my position have to be. It comes with the territory. Once you relax, that's when you get a bullet in the back of your head.

I'm not looking for anything in particular as I rake my eyes over the landscape below—just observing like the predator I am—when my eyes suddenly light on a figure that makes me go completely still. My chest tightens inexplicably.

Dios mio, she's the most beautiful creature I've ever seen. She's a petite thing with long chestnut hair that flows down to her impossibly tiny waist. I don't know what it is about her that draws my eyes to her, but I can't seem to tear them away from her. I'm like a magnet being pulled to my polar opposite. Something about her is drawing me to her.

She's wearing leggings and an off-the-shoulder top that's stylishly too large for her small frame. She hurries along the sidewalk, her hair flowing out behind her. She's effortlessly beautiful with her pale skin that looks like porcelain. I'm dying to see her eyes, and my wish is granted when she suddenly turns and looks in my direction.

Of course, she's not looking at me because she can't see through these windows, but it feels like she is. I run a hand over my aching chest as I look directly into her eyes. They're a pure green and shimmering like the most perfect emeralds. Framed by dark lashes, they're sparkling with innocence. My eyes trail down over an upturned nose to sinfully puffy lips.

She gets closer as she crosses the street. My eyes follow her the entire way. I turn my head to follow her path, watching the gentle sway of her hips as she walks into a spa.

I can see through the parlor's window and watch her as she relieves the girl working reception.

I continue to stare at her, watching every movement of her hands as she answers the phone. I watch the way her lips move as she speaks. My own lips tingle as I imagine what those pink lips would feel like underneath mine. What they would taste like.

I stare, mesmerized, as I watch her hair shine and ripple when she pushes it back over her shoulder gracefully.

She's completely captivating.

I suddenly need to know everything about her. I've never reacted to a woman this way, and I can have any woman I want. I know that, though I've never made much use of the privilege. It just comes with the territory. As the prince of the mafia and next in line to inherit the empire, I've got enough money and power to have my pick of women, but I've never wanted one.

Until now.

With my attention still fixated on my little *tesoro*, I

dial a number on my phone. My head of security answers on the first ring.

"Yeah. Give me everything you can find on the receptionist who's currently working the desk at the massage parlor on Fifth. I want all the details forwarded to me ASAP."

I scowl when Rocco finally shows up, and I have to tear my eyes away from my *tesoro*. It takes everything within me not to glance back over at her, but I know men in our profession look for any weakness, and I don't want to put my angel on anyone's radar.

She's mine, and *only* mine.

Grace. Her name is Grace. Grace Birmingham. My little Gracie. Eighteen years old. Barely legal. Probably too young for my twenty-eight-year-old ass, but ask me if I give a fuck.

She lives alone in a shitty apartment building on a side of town an angel like her doesn't belong in. I don't know how she lucked into the job as a receptionist at the massage parlor, but it's enough for her to pay her own rent and utility bill—barely.

I trail my thumb over my lip as I sit outside her apartment building, staring up at the open window. I can see her sitting on her couch with her feet curled up underneath her. She's reading a book, and my eyes are trailing over the exposed skin of her bare legs. She's wearing a pair of shorts that clings to every curve of her ass and legs. Her tank is too short and bares a bit of her midriff.

Part of me is angry that she's dressed like that and sitting there with her window blinds open for every pervert who walks by to stare up at her. Another part of me is thankful for the view so I can feast my eyes on her.

I keep my gaze fixed on her as I consider the interesting information my man pulled up on Grace Birmingham—or rather, the lack thereof.

I have the best resources money can buy, yet he couldn't find any record of Grace's parentage. She's listed as an orphan. She reportedly showed up at the orphanage when she was barely two years old, and she's been there ever since. No papers. No nothing. It's like her parents never existed. It's like *she* never existed until the orphanage took her in and gave her a new identity.

Who are you, Grace Birmingham?

I watch as she runs a finger through her hair. She finally closes the book, stands, and stretches languorously like a little kitten.

My cock hardens, and I palm myself through my slacks as my eyes trail over her tight, young body.

I could take her right now, but I'll wait. I know once I make my move, I'll have to lock her away. There's a reason a man in my position can't have a woman. Women make us weak. Women become a pawn to be used against us, and I can't make Gracie a target.

No, I'll bide my time. Let her live her life in oblivion a while longer, but once everything is ready, she'll be mine.

Grace

I paste a smile on my face and internally count to ten instead of doing what I really want to do, which is take this pen and stab Sherry's smug face in the eyeballs. I swear the other woman who works reception here at the massage parlor is such a bitch. I don't know what she has against me, but I remind myself that I won't be doing this forever. Somehow, I'm going to save up enough money to get out of here. Maybe I just need to get out of the city, period.

I close my eyes and picture a little green lawn with no neighbors in sight. Well, maybe one or two houses. I just don't want to be caged in on all sides like I am here in my apartment in the city where I have to smell all the varied cuisine everyone in the building cooks at all hours of the day and night.

I don't need anything big or fancy. Just a small little cottage will do. It doesn't even have to have a white picket fence. I'm not that picky. I just want my own little place. Maybe I can learn to grow my own food and be sustainable on my own. Yeah, that would be super zen.

For the moment, though, I'm grateful for this job because at least I make enough to have my own place without having to have a roommate. I don't make much more than that. I'm pretty much scraping by paycheck to paycheck, so I don't know how I think I'm going to save up enough for my little dream cottage out in the country, but first things first. Survival.

Everything else will come eventually. I can't give up. Hope is what has gotten me through my entire life.

You would think all of my hope would be crushed by now growing up parentless in an orphanage, but I've always held on to a bit of hope. Oh, it's not hope in the goodness of humanity. I've seen firsthand how shitty humans can be. Now I'm holding out hope in myself that I can overcome my challenges. So far, I have, and I'm damn proud of myself for it.

I don't let anyone get too close because that only leads to disappointment. But I don't think I'm as jaded or bitter as many of the kids who grow up without parents. I still see the good in the world. I think.

I'm getting ready to close. I'm the last person left at the shop, and it's my job to close up two nights a week. I get up to go lock the door before I return to the desk to shut down the computer and close out everything.

When I turn around from locking the door, I gasp and jump back when a man is towering over me. My eyes trail up, up, up until they meet the most startling blue I've ever seen in my entire life. The crystal-clear blueness of his eyes only stands out in stark contrast to his jet-black hair. It's full on the top and waves back from his face stylishly.

The man is huge and obviously muscular. It's all the light button-up shirt underneath his suit coat can do to contain the hard pecs of his chest. His thighs are like cannons, and oh my god, I try not to look, but my eyes can't help skimming over the clearly well-endowed thing he's packing between his legs.

His mildly tanned olive skin tone speaks to a Mediterranean ethnicity, and when he opens his mouth and speaks, I immediately pinpoint him as Italian.

His accent isn't overly pronounced. His English is quite good. It's more the words that he uses.

"Hello, *tesoro*." I don't know what *tesoro* means, but I recognize it as an Italian word.

His voice is deep and smooth as velvet. It slides over me sensuously. I stare up at him like a deer caught in the headlights before I finally shake my head and get my wits back about me. What the hell is wrong with me? This man just appeared out of nowhere, and I'm alone with him in a darkened office. Why aren't warning bells going off in my head? Instead, I'm standing here ogling him and in awe of how hot he is.

"How did you get in here?" I ask him. "Who are you?"

He chooses not to answer the first question. Instead, he only addresses the latter. "Massimo Russo."

"We're closed," I tell him with a shaky voice as I take a cautious step back closer to the desk.

He doesn't miss a beat. His eyes never waver from me as he bridges the distance between us. "I know. I came to see you."

"Me?" I squeak, wincing when I sound like a frightened mouse. I clear my throat. "Do I know you?"

What a stupid question. Of course, I don't know him. If I'd ever seen a man like him, there's no way I could forget him. His image has already been burned into the back of my retinas.

"No, but I know you, *tesoro*." He reaches out slowly as if I'm an animal that he doesn't want to spook before his hand gently cups my cheek.

I can't help it. I close my eyes and lean into his touch. I'm not one for being touched. I wasn't the girl who had loving parental figures giving her hugs and raining kisses down upon her. I've never had any boyfriends either. I saw too many other orphans looking for affection and then ending up pregnant as a result, and I didn't want that to happen to me.

So, I don't know if it's just him or the absence of touch in my life that has my skin tingling at the contact, but I suspect it's just *him*.

He strokes his thumb gently over my cheek, and when I open my eyes, his blue orbs are blazing down at me intently like a roaring blue fire.

His phone chirps, and I sense his irritation at

being interrupted as he pulls it out of his pocket. He frowns down at the screen, and his face has turned stony when he looks back up at me, a hint of regret in his eyes. "I'm sorry, but I have to go now."

His hand comes up to cup my cheek again. His face looms closer to mine as he brings his lips down until they're just a hair's breadth from mine. They're so close I can feel them skimming across my lips as he whispers, "Be a good girl until next time."

"Next time?" I expel the words in a breathless rush, but he's already turned and is walking away from me. All I can do is stand there, my entire body trembling as I gape after him.

When he reaches the door, he turns back and orders me, "Lock this back immediately."

It's like I'm in a trance. I immediately move to obey him.

He nods at me in approval, his eyes blazing down into mine through the glass one last time before he turns and strides over to a waiting vehicle. He gets in the backseat, and I watch in a daze as the darkened vehicle pulls away from the curb, my mind still reeling.

What the hell was that?

Chapter Two

Massimo

INCOMPETENT. Every fucking one of them. I swear to God, I'm going to fire every last man working in this warehouse.

"How the hell did Doyle's men get past our guys?"

The moron on the other end of the line sputters as he tries to come up with an excuse.

"Never mind!" I snap at him. "Just contain it for fuck's sake."

I grip the phone in my hand so tightly I hear the case crack. I was interrupted with my little Gracie for *this*. This fucking territorial bullshit. Doyle better hope

I never get my hands on him because I'll wring his fucking neck for all the aggravation he's caused me.

The head of the Irish mafia has been a pain in our asses for as long as I can remember, but he's gotten cocky lately. Now he's encroaching on our territory, and my father is so livid about it, I'm surprised he hasn't given himself a heart attack over it. Just the mention of Conner Doyle's name is enough to raise his blood pressure so high that his face turns red as a beet.

The Irishman is our biggest enemy, and he's getting bolder, but he's slipperier than an oiled snake. He's always just out of our reach. To make matters worse, he has no family to speak of—no wife or children—so no weaknesses to exploit to draw him out.

No, he sits protected behind a wall of security and keeps sending his lowest men to antagonize us.

But he's going to slip up one day, and when he does, I'll be there. And I'm going to make him pay double for interrupting me when I finally got to meet my little *tesoro* in the flesh.

I feel my skin vibrate just thinking about her. Maybe it was premature for me to show myself to her now, but I couldn't take it anymore. I had to touch her, be near her, smell her. Her sweet berry scent still fills my nostrils, and I can still feel how petal soft her skin felt beneath my fingertips. Her lips were so pink, so *ripe*.

I *need* to taste her.

Soon, I promise myself. Soon, she'll be completely *mine*.

It's killing me not being able to be near my little Gracie. Everything's ready to go on my end, except for fucking Doyle raising hell and starting a war. As much as I'm dying to take Gracie for myself right now, I know that now isn't the best time. I can't take her in the middle of a war and put her in danger like that. If people find out she means something to me, she'll become a target.

Still, I can't stop myself from watching her every spare moment I get. I have cameras put up inside her little apartment and everywhere she frequents. I make sure I have a camera on her at all times. I watch her as she walks to and from work. I have a tracking device installed on her phone so I can pull up the app on my phone and pinpoint her at any moment. I have this obsessive need to know where she is at all times.

When I close my eyes and dream, it's her pretty green eyes I see shimmering up at me while I'm bent over her, stroking myself in and out of her, listening to her beautiful cries and whimpers as she falls apart on my cock.

I wake up humping my pillow like a rabid beast more times than I can count, and I don't even care. When I wake up in that half-dozing, half-awake, dream-like state and realize what I'm doing, I continue right on fucking my pillow, imagining it's her until I squirt sticky ropes all over it. That's how desperate and hard up I am for her.

I've never felt this way about another woman. In the past, women were a dime a dozen. I won't go so far as to call myself a player, but I'm no virgin. In my younger days, I explored and had my share of women, but lately, all I've needed was my hand to take care of my needs.

Until Grace, that is.

Now she consumes my thoughts. I can't get off without picturing her beautiful green eyes, her tight little body, and even when I do nut harder than I've ever nutted in my entire life, I'm still not satisfied. I'm always aching for more, and I know the only thing that will satisfy me is the real thing. *Grace.*

Even then, I suspect that one time won't be enough. If I ever get one taste of her, I'll want more and more and more—like a heroin addict. One hit will never be enough. It'll just fuel the desire for more. Like an alcoholic, I'll have to have more and more to get my fix. I inherently know that.

Which is another reason I know it's not wise for me to be around her. I'm barely hanging on to my control by a thread.

It eventually gets to be too much, and I can't take it anymore. Just one hit. That's all I need. That's what I tell myself anyway as I sit outside her office on one of the nights that she closes. I don't like her walking home alone in these darkened streets anyway, even though I'm always there in the shadows watching over her for in case something happens. I'd feel safer if she was in my vehicle with me.

That's why when she comes out, I'm leaning against the back of my vehicle while my driver sits in the front, awaiting my orders. "Hello, Grace."

She jumps and spins toward me with a little gasp, her green eyes going wide when she sees me. "You!" she says with surprise.

I can't exactly say I sense fear in her. It's more like an anxiousness or excitement.

I stalk over to her slowly, a smile curving my lips and my heart hammering as I get nearer to her and her sweet, berry scent washes over me. I feel my core settling and my shoulders relaxing at finally being near her again.

This woman...I need her.

"Ah, you remember me."

She blinks up at me. "Of course I remember you." She speaks softly, cautiously.

"And who am I?" I prompt her as my eyes rake over her, drinking her in.

She licks her lips nervously, and I fight back a groan as my eyes home in on her little tongue sliding across the puffy pink flesh of her lips.

"The man who somehow got into the office the other night and said he knows who I am," she whispers.

"My name, *tesoro*," I prompt her, needing to hear it spoken in her breathy little voice. She has yet to say my name, and I'm dying to see if it sounds the same way in real life as it does in my fevered dreams.

"Massimo," she whispers.

I close my eyes and savor the musical sound of the syllables rolling over her tongue. My name so softly spoken in her husky little voice floods my senses, sounding even better than I ever imagined.

"Get in the car, *tesoro*," I order her gently yet sternly.

Her brow furrows. "What?"

I motion to my idling vehicle. "Let me drive you home."

She hesitates like a rabbit caught in a snare and looks between me and the car, weighing her options.

I take another step toward her to close the remaining distance between us and reach out to gently cup her cheek. Silky soft. I feel a tremble pass through her. Her lips part and her breathing quickens so that her little chest is heaving up and down.

She looks up at me with those emerald green eyes, and I see the desire hidden in their depths. She senses the predator in me. She senses the danger and power, but she's drawn to me—just like I am her.

"Come on, Gracie," I croon to her, coaxing her gently as I take her hand and begin pulling her over to the vehicle, my skin buzzing where our palms touch.

She glances behind her as if someone is going to come and save her, but I tighten my grip on her hand. *No one is going to take you away from me, tesoro.*

When she turns back to me, it's with resignation in her eyes. She swallows and gives me a brief nod. Victory swells my chest as I open the door and help her into the car before sliding in next to her.

I close the door with finality.

Finally, I have her all to myself.

I'm not going to waste a single moment either.

* * *

Grace

After a week of seeing his face in my mind every time I close my eyes, here he is again.

Massimo.

He's just as dark and handsome as I remember with an aura of power and danger pulsing around him.

He has that kind of self-assurance about him that only men with great power have. His tone was commanding when he told me to get in the vehicle, even though it wasn't harsh, though he made it clear that I didn't have a choice in the matter.

And there must be something wrong with me because something about that tone caused my nipples to pebble in my bra. They're still hard and aching, and I feel a pulse in between my legs. He slides into the back of the vehicle and places his arm over the seat behind me. He doesn't leave hardly any space between our bodies. I'm practically in the crook of his arm as his big frame seems to suck all the air out of the backseat.

His masculine scent wraps around me. He smells expensive, like sandalwood and mahogany and one-hundred percent virile male, and my God, he's ripped too. I can see the muscles in his thighs ripple and cord when he moves.

Everything about him is large. I'm teeny tiny anyway, but I feel even smaller sitting next to his gigantic form.

He doesn't ask me where I live before he tells the driver my address. I blink, though I'm not entirely shocked at the knowledge that Massimo knows where I live. He said he knew me even though I didn't know him, and I feel a tingle go up my spine as I realize what this means.

I lick my lips as I ask him nervously, "Have you been stalking me?"

Massimo's piercing blue eyes capture mine. He stares at me for a long moment as if he's drinking in my face and committing it to memory before he finally answers me. "I have been watching over you, my little *tesoro*."

I swallow. "So that's a yes? Because that's the definition of stalking, right? Watching someone without their knowledge?"

Massimo simply shrugs his shoulders unapologetically. "Call it what you will, Gracie."

Gracie.

No one has ever called me that before. I've never let anyone get close enough for them to develop a nickname or pet name for me. I shouldn't like it. I don't know anything about this man, but I can't deny that I like the way he calls me Gracie. The way it sounds in the deep timbre of his voice.

He traces a finger along my thigh, and I can feel his touch burning me through the cotton of my leggings. I swallow again—hard. "What do you want from me?"

He tips my chin up and forces me to look at him so that he's looking directly into my eyes when he answers, "I want so much with you, Grace Birmingham."

My heart is pitter-pattering away in my chest as he lowers his head down to mine. My breath hitches in my throat. I close my eyes, anticipating his kiss, but it never comes. When I open my eyes, it's to find his eyes open, staring right into mine. His lips are so close to mine, I can feel his breath fanning across them. "So beautiful," he murmurs, the word skating across my lips.

He threads a hand through my hair and drags it through the silky strands, watching his hand pass through it as if it mesmerizes him.

His nostrils flare, and he leans in toward me again.

I'm certain that he's going to press his lips against mine this time, but he simply reaches across me and pops open the door.

When he finally sits back, I can breathe again, though I'm both strangely relieved and disappointed that he didn't kiss me.

I look up to see his eyes blazing that blue fire down at me. "Go inside, *tesoro*, and make sure you lock the door behind you."

I stare at him for a moment longer, frozen in place, before I finally break myself out of whatever trance he put me in and step out of the back of the vehicle on shaky legs.

I can't tell if his order was a warning that I should be worried that I'm in danger from someone else—or from him.

Chapter Three

Grace

OF COURSE, after I'm safely in my house with the door locked like Massimo told me, my mind obsessively replays our every interaction from the first one down to this last one, and I think of all the things I wish I'd asked him and said to him.

I'm notorious for that, for overanalyzing things after the fact and thinking of better ways I could have responded. It seems like so far my modus operandi around Massimo is to freeze up and wordlessly obey every order the man gives me.

I don't know what it is about him, but I should be more afraid knowing that a man like him is watching me. I should have asked a hell of a lot more questions and been more outraged at his order to take me home. What kind of idiot am I to get into the car with a man I don't even know? Yeah, I know his name, but that's about it.

I don't know why I never thought to do it before, but I fire up my laptop and type Massimo's name into the search bar. My eyes widen when the results pop up. He's the son of the city's most notorious crime lord, Vitale Russo. According to the searches, Vitale is the head of the Italian Mafia here in the States, which means that Massimo is the mafia prince who's set to inherit his father's throne. He's an only child, so he's the only heir to the criminal empire.

That explains the aura of darkness and power that seems to surround him. My heart drops. How the hell did I garner the attention of the mafia prince?

I may not have had strong parental guidance growing up, but I've lived in the city long enough to know that Massimo is not the kind of man an innocent young girl should get involved with. He's too dangerous.

But, wait, it's not like I *am* involved with him. I haven't done anything to encourage him. The man just admitted to watching me and keeps showing up out of nowhere whenever it suits him. And despite the dangerous vibes he gives off, I don't feel like he would hurt me.

The way he looks at me, I think I know what he wants from me, and my cheeks flush at the knowledge, especially when I have to acknowledge that my traitorous body wants that too.

I haven't been able to get my mind off the man since the first night he somehow made his way into the massage parlor undetected and assaulted me with those fiery blue eyes.

I close my laptop and stare into the darkness of my studio apartment as I chew on my lips. Maybe he will just leave me alone if I tell him once and for all that I'm not interested. Yeah, I have no interest in getting involved with him. I want a simple life with my own little cottage out in the country, and that will never happen if I stay on the mafia prince's radar. Hell, I don't even know how I got there, but I couldn't be unluckier because Massimo is so not the type of man whose attention I want on me.

I nod my head to myself as if it's all settled. Yes, that's what I'll do. If Massimo shows up again, I'll just tell him as politely as I can to please leave me alone. Surely, he will if I ask him nicely?

* * *

My mind might know what's best for me, but my subconscious obviously doesn't because when I fall asleep, I dream of fiery blue eyes hovering over me.

I wake up sweating and aching and frustrated. I know some girls touch themselves to relieve aches, but I've tried that before and I've never been able to reach that pinnacle of pleasure.

I try to go back to sleep, but it's to no avail. My body is throbbing with need, so I finally kick off my covers and put my hands under the band of my panties. I rub my aching clit in little circles, my eyes closed as I replay the images from the dream I just had. Massimo's fiery blue eyes blaze down on me. His lips skate over my skin. His breath is in my ear as his body strokes in and out of me.

I feel the pressure between my legs building and building higher than it ever has before. I imagine his blue eyes again and hear the way he calls me Gracie in that deep, velvety voice. Tingles shoot throughout my body from that point I'm stroking, and I arch my hips up into my hand, chasing the feeling. "Massimo!" I gasp out his name as my entire body convulses and I'm suddenly wracked with pleasure so intense that I momentarily see stars.

I have to stop rubbing myself as moisture floods my fingers and my swollen bud becomes too sensitive to withstand touch. I fall back against the bed and stare up at the ceiling with wide eyes, my lips parted in awe.

So *that's* what it feels like. If feels that good on my own, what would it feel like with a man's cock inside of me? With Massimo's cock inside me?

My face flames when I realize Massimo was the mental stimulation I needed to get off.

Massimo.

The mafia prince.

The dangerous man who I have no business messing around with.

The powerful man whose attention I don't want.

I am so fucked.

* * *

Massimo

"Fuck!" I groan as I tug on my swollen dick furiously. Watching Grace play with her sweet little pussy while moaning my name was enough to have me harder than a steel rod. My cock rose to attention so fast I'm surprised the fucker didn't bust clean through my pants.

I grunt as I shoot my load into my open palm, making a mess all in my office. I don't even give a fuck. Grace moaning my name while her fingers flew over her little clit is more than I can take.

I saw the look of wonder on my little Gracie's face. She looked shocked at what just happened, and then it hits me like a knife. That was Grace's first orgasm, which can only mean one thing. My little *tesoro* is a virgin.

That knowledge fills me with a sense of possessive urgency. The need to claim pulses through my entire being. I'm like a lion in mating season. The need to go over there and stuff my cock in her before some other male does is so strong, I have to grit my teeth to fight it.

I already knew that there wasn't any evidence of a boyfriend in her life and that she doesn't seem to date, but I had never dared hope that she would be completely untouched. Mine in every way.

But it makes sense that she is purity itself with the bright innocence shining out of her eyes. She's too good to be true. Perfect in every way.

Mine.

My new knowledge makes me even more anxious

to hurry up and have her with me. I call my captain to get an update on where we are with Doyle's slimy ass. "I don't care what you have to do. We need to catch this fucker pronto," I snap at him, irritated that we're the most powerful crime organization in the world with more resources than the fucking President of the United States, yet we can't seem to pinpoint one Irish motherfucker—an Irish motherfucker who is getting in the way of me claiming my little *tesoro* for myself.

I don't know how long I watch her as she falls asleep immediately after her orgasm. She lays with the covers still thrown off of her, her tank top ridden up to expose an expanse of smooth stomach. I can still see the wet spot staining her little cotton panties and my cock starts getting hard all over again.

Fuuuck. I'm going to have a permanent case of blue balls before this is all said and done.

I can't catch that motherfucking Doyle soon enough.

I stroke a finger over Grace's sleeping form on the screen. *Soon, tesoro. Just hold on. I will come for you soon.*

* * *

It's a week before I get to see my little *tesoro* in the flesh again. Doyle is wreaking so much havoc throughout our city that it takes all my time, attention, and resources to try to contain the mess he's making. So, I have to content myself with watching my little Gracie over camera feeds.

It's not enough, though, and I'm jonesing for another hit. I need to smell her fresh berry scent and feel her petal soft skin underneath my fingertips to tide me over.

She's locking up again tonight. I've already snuck into the massage parlor ready to surprise her. She goes over to shut and lock the door, but a man hurries up to it and knocks. She must know him because she opens the door.

I clench my jaw as I watch their interaction. "Hey, babe," he greets her. I grind my molars together at the endearment. How does she know this fucker?

"Can I help you, John?" she asks, peering up at him. The fucker is tall but not as tall as me and not nearly as bulky.

"Yeah," he grins down at her, his eyes raking over her delectable little body. My fists clench now with the sudden urge to rip those eyeballs from his head so he'll never be able to look at *mi princesa* that way again. "I need to book something. I didn't know if I would get here in time."

"You know you can always book with us over the phone or through the app," she points out.

He shrugs like the entitled asshole he is. "I know, but I was in the area and thought it would be easier just to walk in here and do it personally."

Oh, I bet you did, asshat. My lip curls up into a snarl.

Grace turns around and motions him to come to the desk. "Well, we're technically closed, but since you're already here, let me pencil you in. Who are you wanting to see?"

"Well, seeing as how you still don't give massages, I guess Rachel will do." He winks at her flirtatiously. *That's it. This fucker is dead.*

She smiles at him cordially but doesn't flirt back. *Good girl.* Her lack of interest calms me a bit.

It's quiet as she jots something down on a post-it note, the only sound in the parlor the light scratching of the pen across the paper. "Okay, I've got you written down. I'll put it in the computer in the morning. I've already closed everything out tonight."

"No problem, baby," he says as he takes a step toward her. I grind my teeth again in irritation. So, we've gone from *babe* to *baby* now?

He continues walking toward her, and I see her eyes widen as he comes around the desk. "Is there anything else I can help you with, John?" The trepidation is clear in her voice. She's starting to pick up on the fact that this motherfucker isn't just here to book an appointment.

"Yeah, there is," he tells her as he licks his lips, a lascivious look in his eyes. "You could agree to that date I've been asking you to go on for forever."

I'm fucking furious now. So, she knows this asshole is interested in her? He's asked her out before, yet she still let him in here tonight when she's all alone? I'm pissed as hell she put herself in danger this way.

She sighs and takes a step back, shaking her head. "I'm sorry, John, but I've told you every time you've asked. I'm not interested."

John's not taking no for an answer, though. I can read the intent clear as day in his eyes even if she can't. He reaches out a hand and touches her arm, and that's when I lose it. I don't think. I just react. I pull the gun from my breast pocket and wordlessly step from the shadows. I fire the gun. The man screams and clutches at his arm, wailing like a little girl as he crumbles to his knees.

Grace gasps and whips around in the direction the shot came from, her eyes widening when she sees me standing there. "You!"

"We're really going to have to work on you

remembering my name, *tesoro*." My voice is dry, but I'm so angry I'm beyond livid.

"Why did you shoot him?" She's indignant on his behalf, and a surge of jealousy surges through me, hot and pulsing.

"He put his hands on you," I growl. "Nobody touches what's mine."

Her mouth parts, but she doesn't step away from me whenever I close the distance between us and place a firm grip on her arm. I look down at the piece of shit still squirming and writhing in pain on the floor in front of us.

"It's just a flesh wound," I reassure him nonchalantly. "You'll live if you forget everything that happened here tonight—most importantly, if you forget you ever knew Grace Birmingham. You got that?"

He nods up at me pitifully. "Yes, whatever you say. Just don't kill me."

My lip curls as I look down at him wriggling on the floor like a worm. There's nothing that disgusts me more than a prick who can't man up and take his punishment with dignity. Fucking coward. He isn't worthy of her. "Her name never leaves your lips again," I instruct, my tone menacing. "You don't come near her. If you see her on the street, you don't look at her. You turn and go the other way. Don't even think about thinking about her. Are we clear?"

"Crystal," the man grits out.

"Count to two hundred and then get up out of here and get to the nearest hospital," I order him.

He nods his head in understanding, but I don't really give a fuck if he obeys or not.

My hands still wrapped firmly around Grace's upper arm, I steer her out of the door and into my waiting vehicle.

It looks like plans have changed.

Chapter Four

Grace

MASSIMO PRACTICALLY DRAGS me to the back of his waiting vehicle. He shoves me into the backseat before he folds his big body down gracefully behind me and slams the door shut. "Drive," he snaps at his driver. The driver must hear the urgency in Massimo's voice because he immediately punches the car into gear and takes off zipping down the street.

My mind is still reeling from everything that just happened as I try to process it all and catch up.

"What the fuck, Massimo?" My voice sounds shrill even to my own ears.

Massimo glances over at me and frowns. "Don't curse," he berates me.

I let out an incredulous laugh. He just shot a man, and yet he has the audacity to reprimand me for cursing?

I look out the window, my heart fluttering when I see that we're not going toward my apartment. "Where are you taking me?" A tingle of warning goes up my spine.

"Somewhere you'll be safe."

His tone brooks no argument, but I snap my head back to look at him and argue, anyway. "I want to go home." I state my demand firmly.

Massimo doesn't speak. He just presses his lips into a thin line.

"Massimo?" I prompt him.

He still doesn't look at me or speak.

"Take me home," I try again.

He expels a heavy breath before he finally turns and looks at me, his eyes blazing. "No," he says firmly. "Since you obviously cannot recognize danger when it's right in front of you, you're coming home with me where you belong." His tone is clipped, his eyes burning in anger.

I just stare at him, my mouth hanging open. This cannot be happening. He's angry at me? Like any of this is my fault! "Are you kidnapping me?"

Massimo doesn't answer. He just tightens his jaw as he holds my gaze defiantly.

I don't know why I'm so surprised. Isn't this the next logical step up from stalking? After stalking, kidnapping? Isn't that what stalkers do? They watch their prey before they finally pounce?

"Massimo, you can't do this," I try to reason with him. Oddly enough, my fear isn't really that he will hurt me so much as I'm bucking against having my freedom ripped away from me.

"I can do whatever I want," he says coolly before he adds with a smirk, "or do you not know who I am by now?"

My cheeks flush as I realize he knows I looked him up. Of course, he knows. Isn't that a stalker's job? To know everything about the person they're stalking?

I shake my head, "Please, Massimo," I beg him. "I don't want this."

Massimo's eyes soften as he reaches out a hand to cup my cheek. A shiver runs down my spine at the contact, and I tremble beneath his touch against my will. "Oh, *tesoro*, you don't know what you want," he tells me softly as he strokes his thumb along my cheekbone before he trails it over my bottom lip. My breath hitches as I stare up into the twin blue flames of his eyes.

This is not normal. This cannot be normal for a kidnapping victim to react to her captor this way. He hasn't even gotten me to wherever he's taking me, and I think Stockholm Syndrome is already setting in. Hell, I think it set in the first moment I saw him. That has to be what this is because I should have reported him to the police the night he essentially broke into the massage parlor and assaulted me. Of course, he didn't hurt me. It's more like he assaulted me with his dark, handsome, masculinity and those blazing blue eyes. Yes, those eyes are what assaulted me, pulling me into their orbs and washing over me with intensity, branding me so that I'd never be the same again.

"No, *mi princesa*," he repeats softly as eyes roll over my face. He takes in my trembling body. His voice is deep and soft and husky. "You don't know what you want. Yet."

He stares at me a moment longer, a heated look in his eyes, before he drops his hand from my face and pulls his buzzing phone up to his ear, answering it in Italian. He holds my gaze captive for another moment before he finally turns his head, releasing me from his hold and effectively dismissing me and giving his full attention to whomever he's on the phone with.

No sooner do I feel dismissed does he lay his big hand on my thigh as if to let me know that I'm still on his mind. His touch brands me through our clothing, and I swallow hard.

I glance back over at Massimo to find his eyes trained back on me again. A lock of his dark hair falls on his forehead, and my fingers itch to brush it back. I clench my hands together tightly in my lap as I work to steady my breathing. I turn my head and look out the window to avoid his gaze.

Dear God, please help me.

Massimo

Every time I get my little *tesoro* to myself, something happens with Doyle or one of our warehouses, pulling my attention away from her. Doyle is a dead man if I ever catch him. Of course, he was anyway in my father's book, but I'm going to make him suffer now for the inconvenience he keeps causing me. No one keeps me away from my little *tesoro*, yet Doyle keeps effectively doing just that, and make no mistake about it. He will pay for it too.

My driver pulls into the private building I own in the city. I bought out an entire high rise, and my penthouse is on the very top floor, so I have a magnificent view of the entire city. I'm hoping that Grace will love it since this is going to be her new home whether she likes it or not.

I already did some digging on the pipsqueak who was trying to force her to go out with him back at the massage parlor, and while it doesn't appear he has any rival associations—or any associations to any criminal organizations for that matter—the point is moot. Seeing another man's hands on my little Gracie prompted me to action. I'm not going to take any further chances with her safety. She's a treasure, a rare jewel, and it's a wonder no man has stolen her yet— and I'm going to make it so that no man does. None other than myself, that is.

I open the door and step out of the back of the vehicle, holding my hand back in to help Grace out. She places her little hand in mine, and I can't help the rush of victory that swells my chest when she voluntarily places her hand in mine.

Of course, that satisfaction is quickly crushed whenever she steps foot onto the pavement and then tears her hand from my grasp and takes off running. I don't know where she thinks she's running to. There's no way out of this garage except through the way we came in—which has already been closed off—or the elevator leading up to my penthouse, and that elevator is secure. Only my key card will activate it.

Still, something within me thrills at the chase, and I take off after her. I catch her in just a few seconds and drag her against me with her back against my chest, my arms banding around her. She's trembling in my hold like a frightened rabbit, and I can't help turning my nose down to the nape of her neck and inhaling her fresh berry scent.

My cock immediately surges to life and reaches out for her body, pressing against her sweet ass through our clothing.

She's still in panic mode, though, completely unaware of what she's done to my body. She fights and wiggles in my hold, dragging her ass up and down my length, creating a delicious friction that's going to result in me making a mess in my pants if she doesn't stop.

"Gracie," I snap her name like a whip, but she continues to writhe in my grip. I clench my jaw. The pressure in my balls becomes so heavy that I can't control myself. I thrust my swollen cock against her ass as I growl, "If you don't stop, I won't be held responsible for what I do, Gracie."

I don't know if it's my words that finally break through to her or the feeling of me thrusting my hard cock against her ass that gets her attention, but she finally stills in my arms.

I'm halfway disappointed. I'd love nothing more than to ravish her right here on the floor of my parking garage, to hell with the driver. My men know better than to intervene, and they also know when to make themselves scarce.

With an arm wrapped firmly around Grace's shoulder, I lead her over to the elevator, keeping her pressed against my side as we take the elevator up to my suite. I hear Grace's gasp whenever I open the front door and she's presented with the view of the city lights. She's impressed despite herself, and that knowledge pleases me. Anything to make my little Gracie happy.

I slide my hand from her shoulder down to her hand and gently lead her over to the room I had made up especially for her. I watch her reaction as she walks inside and glances around the luxurious room. As much as I'd like to move her immediately into my room, I know she'll need time to adjust. Giving her her own space will give her that sense of normalcy—as much normalcy as she can have in a situation like this, that is.

My chest tightens at seeing her here in the space I prepared for her. I tilt her chin up toward me until I'm looking into her pretty green eyes. I drink her in before I have to leave and go take care of business.

She's like a siren, drawing me in. I can't resist lowering my mouth until it's just a hair's breadth from hers. I let my lips skim lightly over hers, every fiber of my being screaming at me to taste her, take her, but I force myself to pull back. I don't want to start something that I can't finish right now. I know one taste of Grace's lips, and I'll be gone. And, unfortunately, my position demands my attention right now. Fucking business. It's always something.

"Make yourself at home, *tesoro*."

She looks at me like I've lost my mind, but I'm unperturbed. Maybe I have lost it, but I don't give a damn.

I nod over to the phone lying on the bedside table. "If you need anything, call me."

Her eyes brighten with hope before she quickly dims them. I suppress my smirk and don't even bother telling her that the phone is wired to only call out my number and will only receive phone calls from my number. It's a one-way communication to *me* and only me. I don't want my little *tesoro* depending on anyone but me, selfish as it is. She'll find that out soon enough, though.

With one last stroke of her cheek, I reluctantly turn and head to the door. "Oh, and Gracie, don't even bother trying to run from me again. There is no escape, I assure you."

Her lips press together into a thin line, and she shoots daggers at me, her green eyes glittering sharper than the finest-cut emeralds.

While it pains me to see her displeasure, I'm resolute. Her safety is the most important thing now, and there's no safer place for her than here with me. Where she belongs.

I close her door behind me but don't bother locking it. There's no need. I meant what I said. There's no escape for her.

She's mine now.

Chapter Five

Grace

WHEN I HEAR the front door close behind Massimo, I make a beeline for the door to the bedroom. It's not locked, and even though I know it's pointless, I head for the front door. My heart leaps within me when I find that it's not locked either only to plummet back down to my feet whenever I go over to the elevator and find that I can't even summon it up without a key.

He's exactly right. There is no escape. I'm trapped here.

I walk aimlessly around the place that is my new prison. I note somewhat wryly that at least my prison is luxurious. I stand before the floor-to-ceiling windows and look out over the twinkling lights of the city. It's a breathtaking view from way up here. I imagine Massimo standing here, looking out over the city as if he's surveying his kingdom. That's probably how he views it too, seeing as how he's next in line to rule over the criminal underworld of the city. The mafia prince...

I drop my face in my hands and shake my head hopelessly. How did I ever get in this situation? I did nothing to draw his attention. I didn't ask for this. Is it just my fate to be involved in dangerous situations? I stand there wallowing in self-pity for a few minutes longer before I finally start walking around the space, checking out every nook and cranny, looking for any crack in defense, any weakness, although I already know I won't find any.

Massimo is a smart, powerful man. There's no way he has left anything to chance. There's no way he has any breach in his security. If he tells me there's no escape, there's no escape. I've never been one to accept things lying down, though.

After I've exhausted myself sweeping the entire penthouse, including the living room and what I'm pretty sure was Massimo's master bedroom, I make my way back to the room he called mine. There's no way to open any of the windows in this entire penthouse, so I don't even bother with that. Instead, I walk over to the closet and open the door, gasping when I see the vast assortment of women's clothing hanging up. I venture inside slowly and run a finger over the smooth fabrics that I already know will be a perfect match for my size. One quick glance at the designer labels confirms my suspicions. I don't even have to slip one of the garments on. I already know it will probably be hand-tailored to my measurements better than any clothing I own.

My eyes about bug out of my head when I take in the fresh price tags still on them.

Three thousand dollars for one shirt. Twenty thousand dollars for one dress. I don't do more than glance at the shoes neatly displayed in cubbyholes in the wall. One look is enough to let me know they are designer too.

I open one of the built-in drawers and gasp at all the twinkling diamonds and gemstones that meet my eyes. Massimo has spared no expense, and it looks like he's gone to a lot of trouble to set all this up, and I can't help wondering how long he's had this planned.

A shiver goes up my spine. Has he been preparing all of this since that first day I met him—or even sooner? How long has Massimo been watching me?

Was he watching me long before he snuck into the massage parlor and made himself known to me? How did I not feel him watching me?

Instead of being frightened that he *was* watching me, I'm more frightened that I had no clue about it. And that's crazy, right? Shouldn't I fear the stalker himself? The mafia prince... I should be more frightened than I am that this insanely dangerous, powerful man has me in his clutches, and there's not a damn thing I can do about it.

I glance back down at the jewelry that's taunting me from the drawer. I suppose the one thing I have going for me is that Massimo seems to like me. The jewels twinkle. Okay, maybe *like* is putting it mildly. He *really* likes me.

I stand there for a few more indecisive moments, chewing on my lip, before I finally head over to the bathroom to take a shower while I don't have to worry about any unexpected visits from Massimo.

I take my time shampooing and conditioning my hair. I use the luxuriant exfoliating scrub I find in a pretty basket beside the tub. My skin feels baby soft when I get out and rub it down with equally expensive lotion.

I blow dry my hair until it's softer and silkier and shinier than it's ever been. I do all of this while I'm deep in thought, trying to figure out a way out of my situation. It has absolutely nothing to do with me wanting to look pretty for Massimo. I couldn't care less what he thinks of me. In fact, this was probably a mistake. I should probably make myself look as unalluring as possible so maybe he'll have second thoughts and let me go.

Something tells me that won't work with Massimo, though. Something tells me that once he sets his mind on something, he pursues it with dogged determination, but he's my captor, and I'm his captive. There's no way I'll ever be okay with that—despite how tall, dark, and handsome the man may be.

I'm going to find a way to escape, if not through a weakness in his fortress, then by using my brain. I haven't gotten to where I am today without a few street smarts. I might be painfully naïve in some ways, but I'm a quick thinker. I just have to figure out how to outsmart Massimo.

I nod to myself. Yeah, that's what I have to do.

I have a feeling it will be easier said than done.

Massimo

It's late when I get back from handling Doyle's latest catastrophe. Grace is already sound asleep in her bed, and it fills me with a sense of satisfaction at seeing her here in the space I made up for her, wearing the clothes that I bought her, although I smirk when I see she pulled on one of the long T-shirts rather than one of the silky negligees I bought her to sleep in.

I know what she's trying to do. She's trying to make herself less appealing, but it won't work. My little *tesoro* doesn't realize she could wear a brown paper sack and I would still want her. It's not about what she wears. It's not even entirely about how she looks. It's about the innocent soul I see shining out of those beautiful green eyes.

Soft light from the city gleams in through the floor-to-ceiling windows, softly highlighting her beautiful features and casting a gold glint on her silky chestnut hair. I lean down over her and inhale her scent. Even with all the top-of-the-line designer cosmetics I bought her, she still smells like fresh berries—something that I'm immensely glad of. It must just be her natural scent. Fresh, young, ripe. It fits her.

She tosses in her sleep, the covers kicking off of

her. I can see her white cotton panties from where the shirt has ridden up slightly. Her creamy thighs are exposed, and my cock begins to cry, leaking a steady stream of precum as it rises to full mast in my pants. I palm myself through my pants roughly, willing my swollen dick to go down, but when Grace tosses her head on the pillow, her eyes still closed and moans softly, I feel more moisture beading at the tip instead—especially whenever she moans my name in her sleep, arching her little back up as she does so. "Massimo..."

My cock responds like a dog jumping at its owner's call. It presses painfully against my zipper, trying its best to bust through and get to the pussy laid out in front of it. Grace gyrates her hips and arches them up in front of me.

It's obvious what she's dreaming about. *Me. Her. Me inside her.*

I groan. As much as I want to give her what she obviously wants—at least in her subconscious—I could never take a woman who's not lucid enough to make the choice on her own. I may be a lot of things, a criminal, a mafia prince, but I'm no rapist.

The first time my cock is inside Grace, it will be with her fully conscious and admitting that she wants it. There will be no dubious consent.

Still, I am a man, and I can't help but unbutton my pants to allow my cock to spring free. The heavy length falls into my waiting hands, and I begin to stroke in time with Grace's little whimpers and moans.

Her skin is flushed as I stare down at her. I wonder if she's going to cream her little panties right here in front of me. The thought causes a jet of precum to shoot from my tip. My god, I've never been this full before, never had the need to cum like this.

She's groaning and whimpering, and I'm grunting and moaning like a bear in mating season, but I can't help it. Her eyes finally flutter open. She looks up at me dazedly. She gasps as she awakens fully. Her eyes pop open wide when she sees what I'm doing. Fuck, I can't stop now, though. There's no way. If anything, seeing her pretty green eyes watching me as I jerk myself off only gets me hotter.

"Massimo…" she says my name again in that breathy, lust-filled voice, her eyes pinned on my dick.

That's all it takes to send me spiraling over the edge. I feel my release bubbling up from my balls. Her eyes widen as she watches me shoot thick, sticky ropes up into the air. Her mouth falls open in shock, and that only makes me come harder as I imagine what it would be like to slide my cock between her waiting lips.

"Grace," I groan out as I rub out the last of my nut for her eyes only. I continue stroking my jerking length until I'm completely spent. When I finish, Grace is still staring up at me with those wide eyes. She licks her lips in a nervous habit she has, but it sends fire rushing straight to my loins. My half-hard cock hardens again.

Her eyes flicked back down to the appendage between my legs and widen when she sees me getting hard again.

She whispers my name again, and I clench my jaw, fighting against the urge to pounce on her here and now. I want to thrust my cock so deep inside her they'll never be room for another man.

"Go to sleep, Gracie," I tell her instead, my voice rough, "before I lose all control and make your dream come true."

Her face colors as she realizes I know what she was dreaming about. She hurries to roll over in the bed, presenting her back to me and pulling the covers clean up to her chin, confirming what I already knew, though the disappointment still bites at me. She's not ready to admit she wants me, and I won't take her until she is.

I bend down close to her to inhale her sweet scent once again before I leave. I see her body tremble at my nearness, and I whisper near her ear, "You don't have to dream about us, *tesoro*. All you need to do is ask, and I will give you anything you desire. The next time you call out my name in your dreams, you might wake up to more than a spurting cock over you."

I hear her shocked intake of breath, and my cock begins to leak again. With a suppressed groan, I straighten and force myself to leave the room before I go ahead and make good on my words and take her here and now.

Chapter Six

Grace

"WHY DID YOU TAKE ME?"

"Because I wanted you." He states it simply, as that as if it's that simple. He sees something he wants, and he takes it, and maybe it is that simple for him because here I am. He wanted me and he took me.

I push my food around on my plate. We're sitting in his dining room together as if we're a normal couple enjoying breakfast together. Of course, Massimo didn't cook all this food. He has chef-prepared meals delivered to his home every week, and he simply heats them up.

I will say that the food is fresh, though. It's

not frozen stuff, and it tastes as if it was prepared just minutes ago by a gourmet chef. I guess that's one perk of having enough money to buy anything you want. You get convenience and quality.

I poke at the eggs on my plate. I feel Massimo's eyes on me, though I won't look at him.

"Are you not hungry, *tesoro*?"

I don't answer him. I just continue to fluff the eggs on my plate.

"You need to eat." His tone is stern and full of disapproval.

Still, I don't answer him.

"Grace," he growls my name in warning, and I finally look up at him.

"When are you going to let me go?"

His jaw hardens, but he holds my gaze steady as he answers frankly, "Never."

My heart falls.

I stare at him.

He stares back at me.

"You can't do that!" I finally protest. "This is kidnapping."

He doesn't even blink. Of course, in his line of work, he's probably done so much worse that kidnapping is hardly a tick on the board.

"Massimo, this is wrong," I try to appeal to him again.

He suddenly jumps up from his chair, the dishes clattering as he does so. I gasp at his sudden movement, but he's beside me in a flash, towering over me, his blue eyes blazing down into mine. "Wanting you is not wrong, *tesoro*." He drops to his haunches in front of me and peers directly into my eyes as he adds slowly, "And you want me too, whether you'll admit it to yourself or not."

His hand comes out to cup my cheek, and I can't stop the tremble that passes through me.

His heated eyes hold mine captive. He looks at me knowingly. "Your body betrays you every time," he notes softly, his voice deep and husky. "Look at how you tremble when I touch you."

I lick my lips nervously and then immediately regret it when his eyes home in on the motion. I hate him for being right, but I snap back irritably, "How do you know that's not fear?"

I see a flash of pain in his eyes as they slip back up to mime. I don't know why, but seeing that flash of sadness in this powerful man's eyes softens something inside me.

"Is it, *tesoro*?" he asked me quietly.

I find I can't lie to him. "No," I finally whisper and

shake my head.

His eyes burn with that blazing heat again. My heart is pounding a mile a minute in my chest as we just sit there suspended in time, staring into each other's eyes.

Our trance is broken by Massimo's phone buzzing. A look of annoyance passes over his face before he pulls his phone out of his pocket and quickly shoots off a reply to whoever texted him. He straightens with a graceful unfurling of limbs, straightening his shirt sleeves when he's at his full height. I try not to stare at the way his muscles bunch and cord underneath the white button-up with every movement he makes. I may be outraged that Massimo kidnapped me like this, but I'm undeniably attracted to him.

That's why I have to keep my wits about me. Otherwise, it's going to be so easy for me to develop Stockholm Syndrome.

"I have business to attend to, *tesoro*," Massimo tells me regretfully. "I'll return to you as soon as I can. Nothing is off limits to you. This is your home now. Make use of anything you wish. And if you require anything else, let me know, and I'll make sure you have it."

He stares down at me as if he's waiting for some acknowledgment of his words. I can't bring myself to say thank you to my captor, even though the words are on the tip of my tongue, so I settle for a brief nod instead.

It obviously suffices because Massimo takes my hand and pulls me up out of my chair before he pulls me close and does that thing where he puts his nose right against my hair and inhales deeply. He skims his lips over mine as he whispers, "Until tonight, *tesoro*. Be a good girl."

I don't know why he doesn't just kiss me already. It's obvious he wants to.

I blink at the turn my thoughts have taken. Why am I even thinking about that? I don't want him to kiss me. He's my captor. An insanely dangerous man. I'm glad he hasn't kissed me.

That's why whenever I hear the front door snap closed, my shaky legs finally give out on me and I collapse back down into the chair. It's from relief— not disappointment. That's what I tell myself, anyway.

It's hard for me to hate Massimo when he makes sure I'm the most spoiled captive ever. Anything I ask him for he gets me, though of course he's too smart for any of my scheming. I asked him for a computer, and he brought one home that same night, but it's been specially programmed so that I can't communicate in or out of it.

I don't know the particulars about exactly what Massimo does for work every day, but after breakfast, he heads out every morning and often doesn't come back until I'm already asleep. Sometimes I wake up to find him sitting in a chair in the corner staring at me like a black panther stalking its prey. Sometimes he's standing over me, looking down at me, and a couple of times I woke up to feel his weight sitting on the side of the bed as he gazed down at me.

When I become aware of his presence, he always murmurs a soft greeting to me. He runs his fingers through my hair, stroking me like a little kitten until I fall back asleep.

It should definitely creep me out more than it does to wake up and find this man watching me sleep, but on some strange level, it's actually comforting. I've never had anyone care about me enough to watch over me while I sleep, and strangely enough, it makes me feel safe and cherished. I'm starting to believe that when Massimo calls me his little tesoro, he truly means it—that I am his treasure. He certainly treats me like something to be treasured. Even the fact that he has locked me up here, away from the world is kind of a testament to how much he treasures me and wants to hoard me all to himself—as wrong as it may be.

The days alone in his penthouse are long and lonely. At first, I spend all of my time obsessing and plotting my escape, but Massimo is always one step ahead of me. He shut down my idea of contacting someone through a computer, though in all fairness, I didn't really expect that to work. Any time I say I want something, no matter how difficult it seems to obtain, he always gets it for me. I even went so far as to tell him that it was time for my yearly checkup with my gynecologist just as an attempt to get him to let me out of the penthouse, but the man brought my gynecologist to me.

I finally give up on outsmarting Massimo—for the time being, anyway. I begin to relax, and when I'm not obsessively plotting ways to escape him, I find that it actually feels liberating to take my foot off the gas and coast for a while. I don't have to worry about work or how I'm going to pay my bills because I don't have any now. I don't worry about where my next meal comes from because they're all provided for me.

In a strange way, my captivity is freeing. For the first time, I'm able to let someone else make the decisions while I don't worry about anything. When I finally submit to the idea that I'm not going anywhere anytime soon, I allow myself to watch some TV and read some books. I dabble in painting, even though I suck at it. Massimo even bought me a gaming system so that I can try my hand at video games. Anything I want for mental stimulation, he gets me.

And Stockholm Syndrome is truly setting in because Massimo is the only person I ever see. Even though he gets home late at night, as the days go by, I find myself waiting up for him because I want to see him. I want any sort of human contact. I find myself looking forward to seeing him.

We don't talk about his day. I don't ask him because I know he won't tell me the details of what he does during the day, but he wants to know every insignificant little detail of my day, and he's not just humoring me. Massimo truly wants to hear about my latest adventure in painting or the book or movie I watched and what I thought of it. I've never had someone take this much of an interest in me before.

Massimo still hasn't touched me other than to stroke his fingers through my hair or cup my cheek. Sometimes he grazes his lips softly over mine, but he still hasn't kissed me, and I haven't caught him masturbating while looking down at me again.

My cheeks still flame at the memory, and I feel moisture pool between my legs when I recall the way his hand flew over the rigid column of his flesh. I don't know what he's waiting for, and I'm certainly not going to ask because as much as my body might think it wants Massimo's big cock inside it, I've always heard that a girl's first time hurts, so I'm nervous about it. Massimo is big all over, and down *there* is no exception. He's more than well-endowed. He's so big that I'm sure it would split me in half if he stuck it inside me.

Maybe that's why he's holding back. Maybe he knows we won't fit too. The thought fills me with a confusing mixture of relief and disappointment.

I've never worn one of the beautiful little negligees Massimo bought me to sleep in. I always wear one of the big slouchy T-shirts instead. I don't know what draws me to all the pretty lingerie hanging up in the closet tonight, but I can't help gliding my fingers over them and imagining how soft the material would feel against my skin.

Surely, it can't hurt for me to wear some of these finer garments. He did buy them for me, after all. I pull one from the rack and slip it on. It's a deep emerald green. The silk falls mid-thigh, barely covering my ass with the back dipping down low to the curve of my spine. The straps are spaghetti thin, and I feel dainty and luxurious as I let my hair down to cascade around my shoulders.

My face is freshly washed, exfoliated, and moisturized. My skin glows thanks to all the expensive products Massimo stocked the bathroom with. I've never pampered myself as much as I have in my time here with him.

I admire myself in the mirror some more. My lashes are naturally dark, and the lighting of the closet makes my green eyes pop against the emerald-green negligee. I feel pretty, and I can't deny how wonderful the silky fabric feels against my skin, so I reason that there's no harm in wearing it for a little while—until Massimo gets home, that is. I'll change back into one of the big T-shirts before he gets here so he doesn't see me in the sexy lingerie and think I'm inviting anything. My cheeks burn at even sending him that kind of message, so yeah, I can enjoy this luxury for a little while, but I'll make sure I change before he gets home.

With that thought in mind, I crawl into the bed and pick up the latest novel I'm reading, getting lost in the pages as I lay propped up against a pile of fluffy pillows encased in fine Egyptian cotton sheets with the highest thread count money can buy.

Chapter Seven

Massimo

MY ENTIRE BODY is still vibrating with rage at my latest knowledge. My father's man just found out that Connor Doyle has a weakness. All this time of thinking he had no wife or children, nothing or no one to use against him, someone finally found out he had a daughter, one he's had no contact with since the day she was born because he didn't want any of his enemies to find out about her. She doesn't even know he exists. She doesn't know who she really is.

That daughter's name?

Grace Birmingham. Or rather, I guess her true name is Grace Doyle.

It took my father's investigative team so long to find Doyle's weakness because he did an exemplary job of hiding her. Apparently, since I took Grace, he's gotten sloppy in his search for her. My men intercepted one of Doyle's men who was tasked with finding Grace, and they tortured it out of him.

Much to my father's delight—and my despair.

My little Gracie is the daughter of my father's arch-nemesis, *my* enemy.

My father already has all of our men scouring the city for her. Predictably, he wants her brought to him so he can use her to get at her father because despite the fact that the man has never been in Grace's life as a father figure, he must care for her on some basic primal level since he took such care to keep her protected and in the shadows so no one would know about her, not to mention the fact that he seems to have temporarily lost his mind since I took her.

I stop outside Grace's door and lean my head on it. I inhale a deep breath before I exhale it wearily. Of course, I didn't tell my father that I have the girl he's looking for, his enemy's daughter—and the love of my life. My obsession. The only woman I'll ever want for the rest of my life.

I don't know what to do. It's a cardinal sin to disobey my father, the head of the mafia, the head of this family, but there's no way in hell I'm giving him my Gracie.

I slip quietly into the room where she's already sleeping. The covers are pulled up over her breasts, and an open book is lying face down on her chest where she must have dropped it as she fell asleep reading. My chest tightens when I see her chestnut hair fanned out around her shoulders. Her puffy pink lips are parted slightly in her slumber. Her dark lashes lay against her porcelain cheeks. She looks like a little porcelain doll. Pure and innocent. She has no idea who her father is or that he just so happens to be the most dangerous, powerful player in the Irish mafia—and my sworn enemy.

No, my sweet little Gracie is innocent in all this. I stand there drinking her in, torn between my duty and my heart.

Grace tosses in her sleep, kicking the covers off her as she does so. It's like my body has been jolted with electricity when I see what she's wearing. My cock rises to full mast in my pants, and desire licks through me when I take in the emerald-green negligee I bought for her.

It looks more beautiful on her than I ever imagined it would. The silk rides up around her thighs so that I can see the rounded bottom of her ass poking out. She doesn't have any panties on, and her back is bare. The stiffened peaks of her nipples are poking through the front of the fabric. My chest heaves up and down as I struggle to control my desire.

I lose the battle when she arches her hips up slightly and breathes my name in her sleep. "Massimo..."

I'm on the bed in a flash, parting her legs and inhaling her scent deeply before I lave her from gash to clit. I curse. She's soaking wet and so motherfucking sweet. She tastes like strawberries and cream. I groan and suck her in earnest, hollowing my cheeks as I pull her clit into my mouth as I roll my tongue over it.

I hear her gasp as she wakes up, her green eyes glittering down at me. "Massimo!" she breathes my name again as she tilts her hips up in offering. Victory swells my chest, and I roughly pull my cock from my pants and stroke the aching length. Precum is dribbling from the tip, and the fucker is so hard it's sticking straight up.

"What did I tell you would happen if I heard you moaning my name in your sleep again?" I ask her, my voice slurred with lust. "Told you you'd get more than a spurting cock. This time you've got me lapping at that pussy like a hungry dog. And you want it too, don't you, *tesoro*? That's why you wore that flimsy little negligee for me, isn't it? You wanted to drive me fucking insane with desire for you. You wanted me to lose control, didn't you?"

I begin to stroke my cock furiously. Grace is writhing beneath me, pulling on my hair and moaning my name as I continue to eat her out until she gushes her sweet cream all over my face.

Her orgasm triggers my own. She's still arching up into me. Her pussy is convulsing and fluttering. I continue stroking myself as I climb up over her and stick just the tip of my cock inside her—just enough that I can feel her falling apart around me as I come. I haven't popped her little cherry, but I'm inside her, connected to her.

And fuuuck, the feeling of her fluttering pussy kissing my cock detonates something inside me. I splash my cum inside her little hole. I feel it tearing up out of my balls in euphoric rushes. I grunt, part of my brain praying that my seed will find its way inside her to impregnate her. I want to make her mine in every way.

Grace is looking up with me at me with wide eyes as I nut with just the crown of my head inside her. My release triggers another orgasm in her because she arches her hips up into me as she convulses around me harder.

"Fuck!" I growl out as she throws her hips up against me, sliding me deeper inside her until I can feel the barrier of her hymen against the tip of my cock. I still her by grabbing her hips, gritting my teeth at the overwhelming sensation as I continue to pulse new jets inside her.

"Massimo," she whines my name, "please!"

My cock is already rock hard again at the pleading note in her voice. "You want me to fuck you, tesoro?" Grace makes a little whimpering sound, and her cheeks heat.

I fist a hand in her hair as I hover over her, my lips brushing up against hers. I'm vibrating with need, but I hold back. "Say it," I order her. "Tell me you want this, Gracie."

She's silent for a beat before she finally submits. "I want you, Massimo," she breathes out in her husky little voice.

I snap and crash my lips down upon hers, claiming them. I'm finally allowing myself to taste those lips that have been taunting me for weeks now. "You taste better than I ever could have imagined."

She moans into my mouth, and that moan registers straight to my cock. I continue to feast on her mouth as I jam my hips forward and pop her little cherry, stuffing her full of my cock. "You're mine now," I snarl, but I'm unable to contain the beast raging inside me as I pummel my hips against hers, fucking her fast and furiously. I know I'm being too rough for her first time, but I can't slow down.

Grace wraps her arms and legs around me and clings to me as she moans and whimpers in my ear, lighting my blood on fire. "You were made for me, *tesoro*. You're mine now. You hear me? No one is ever going to take you away from me."

"Massimo," she breathes out my name again like it's a prayer, and it's music to my ears.

"Yes, that's it, *tesoro*. Say my name when your pussy is full of me. Who do you belong to?"

She says my name again, her voice a high whine this time. Her breath is coming out in little pants, and I can tell she's getting close. "Look at me, Grace," I order her, my own voice coming out in rough pants.

Her eyes snap open, wild with lust and burning a green fire as I continue to rut up into her. I feel my cock swelling and know that I'm going to come again any moment. "Look at me when I'm balls deep in you and scream my name when you come on my cock. Can you do that for me, *princesa*?"

Grace, good girl that she is, immediately obeys,

holding my eyes as she screams my name. I feel the first flutters of her convulsing around me—hard. It catapults me to my own release. "Gracie!" I roar as I hammer into her harder than before, trying to get as deep as I can. I want to fuck my soul into hers until we are permanently joined as one being.

I come harder than the first time. My spend feels like it's being ripped violently from my balls. My cock pulses inside her over and over again until her tiny womb can't contain it all and my sticky release overflows, sliding down onto my tight balls. I hold myself deep inside her as I continue to come inside her in hot pulses while her pussy flutters around me.

I wrap my arms around her back and gather her against my chest before I roll us so that I'm lying on my back and she's laying on top of me, my cock still buried inside her. Fuck, the way I feel now I don't know if I'll ever pull it out of her. It feels so right to be buried inside her like this. I'm connected to her more than physically. It's like there's this pulsing spiritual bond between us.

A surge of protectiveness wells up inside me as I hold her close. I love the feeling of her slight weight against my chest as I stroke her hair. I kiss her forehead and her cheeks before I softly kiss her lips once again. "*Te amo, tesoro*. I love you, *mi princesa*. You're mine. No one will ever hurt you. I will protect you. Now and always." The promises and endearments come pouring out of me in a flood. I speak in a jumbled mixture of English and Italian, but fuck if I can control it.

Grace Birmingham is my everything. Fuck anyone who tries to come between us—including my father.

Chapter Eight

Massimo

I WAS RIGHT. One taste of her isn't enough. Having her has unleashed a ravenous beast inside me.

I take her several more times throughout the course of the night. I spend at least an hour kissing every inch of her body until she's sighing and moaning and melting up into me. I could spend forever just kissing her sweet lips.

She's laying with her head on my chest now, fast asleep like a little kitten. I pet her hair, marveling at the treasure in my arms. My *tesoro*. My everything. My reason for living.

My jaw clenches involuntarily when I remember

just whose daughter she is. It's not her fault, and I don't hold it against her, but I know my father is going to be relentless in his search of Doyle's daughter if he thinks it will give him a bargaining chip up on the man.

While I've never known my father to be one of those ruthless mafia men who harms women, he's not above exploiting them for his own gain, and his hatred for Grace's father runs so deep that he might even cross that line if he had her in his clutches.

I look down at my sleeping Gracie. What should I do? I consider letting her go, but I immediately shut that idea down. Not only does my heart, body, and soul balk at the thought of being separated from her now, but my rational mind also tells me that there's no place safer for her than under my protection. If anyone can protect her from her father, it's me, the second-most powerful man in the city.

My father might be the most powerful man in the city, but the one thing Grace and I have going for us is that my father doesn't currently know she's in my care —and I intend to keep it that way until I figure out how to handle this mess.

Even if I thought setting Grace free would protect her, I'm not sure I'd be able to do it, greedy bastard that I am. One hit of her and I'm addicted. I curse internally. I knew it would be this way. This woman has me wrapped around her tiny little finger, and she doesn't even know it. I would burn this city to the ground over her.

I press a protective kiss against her sleeping head as I continue to stroke her hair gently, marveling at the way my fingers glide through the silky strands. She's slumbering so peacefully. I completely wore my poor girl out, but I can't help it. I'm insatiable when it comes to her. If I could live with my cock inside her, I would.

My cock begins stiffening again just remembering how well she took me. How she begged her more. Her breathy whimpers and moans and then the way she screamed my name whenever she fell apart all over me.

I hear a knock at my door and frown. No one ever knocks on my door. No one is able to get past my security without my knowledge, which means I never receive any unexpected visitors.

I go completely still when I realize what this means. There's only one man with enough power to pull off something like that. My father.

When his knocking becomes more insistent, I slip out of bed, careful not to disturb Grace. I debate waking her up and telling her to stay put, but I don't want to scare her. She seems to be sleeping deeply anyway, so my best bet is to leave her here and get my father gone before she awakens. It's scarcely five o'clock in the morning, so she shouldn't wake for a while yet. She usually doesn't wake until eight or nine, but I bet she'll sleep later than that after I kept her up all night making love to her and fucking her in turns.

I curse under my breath when my father's pounding becomes even more insistent. I hurriedly tug on a pair of slacks and a shirt before making my way to the front door. I have no doubt he would have barged straight in had he been able to gain access to the key. Unlike the key to my elevator, there's only one key to my actual penthouse, and it's mine. My head of command might have access to my elevator, but he doesn't have access to my internal apartments. I'd never trust anyone that much.

No sooner do I open the door than my father comes storming in. He begins to pace around the living room like a lion. No greeting or anything. He just gets right to it. "Where the fuck is she?" My heart stills within me, and my entire body goes rigid.

If he's found out I've got Grace...

I don't even have a chance to finish that thought before he goes on, "My men have been searching everywhere for her. How hard can it be to find one woman? She's not in her apartment. She hasn't shown up for work in weeks. It's like she disappeared off the face of the earth. I would think Doyle got to her first and got her safely hidden, but my sources tell me he's searching just as hard for her, too."

I take in a deep breath. I'm not sure what I'm going to tell him, but I need to calm him down enough to get him out of my apartment so he doesn't discover Grace is here with me. It's not that I'm above lying to my father, although I honestly don't think I ever have. I've always followed orders. My father and I have always had a respectful relationship, not only business-wise but as a father and a son, but I won't let anyone—including him—come between me and Grace.

Before I get a chance to say anything, a soft voice says, "Oh, I'm sorry. I didn't mean to interrupt, but I thought I heard my name."

My heart trips within me with dread. Grace looks over at me and blushes. She's wearing the emerald-green negligee I removed off of her last night. She must have picked it up from the floor and put it on before she padded out here, and thank god for that. At least she didn't come traipsing in here naked. I glance over at my father and see him staring at her, and the jealous beast within me rises up. I immediately move to step between him and Grace, blocking her from his vision.

My father's eyes turn to me with a look of pride. "If you already had her son, why didn't you just say so?" He chuckles before he adds, "And hell, she is a pretty little thing. If you wanted to fuck her, I'd have let you do that, anyway."

I square my jaw in anger. "Don't talk about her like that," I grit out.

My father's eyes widen before they narrow, and he looks at me suspiciously. "What's going on here?"

I don't answer. I just stand there with my jaw clenched, trying to get control of myself. I could murder him right now for even seeing her in this state of undress.

Grace echoes my father's question. "What's going on, Massimo?" Her voice is shaky. She's clearly scared, and I put a hand behind me to steady her, but I never move from my position in front of her, shielding her from my old man's gaze.

"Go back to your bedroom, Grace." She makes no move to obey me.

My father splays out his hands. "Why send her away, son? Let her stay. Maybe she can answer some of my questions since you seem averse to doing so.

How long have you had her?" he asked me nonchalantly, but my father is no fool. I think he's already put two and two together and figured out that I'm the reason no one has been able to find Grace.

When I don't answer, he directs the question to her. "How long have you been here, sweetheart?"

She opens her mouth and looks to me, but I give her a firm shake of my head. "You don't owe him anything, Grace."

My father looks between us before he directs another question to Grace. "Do you know who you are, sweetie?"

Grace's brows pull down into a frown. "Grace Birmingham," she answers my father like he's crazy. His mouth pulls into a grin as his eyes turn back to me. "She has no idea, does she, son?"

"She has nothing to do with this," I tell him firmly.

My father shrugs. "Maybe not, but she's still the pawn I need to get her father under control."

Grace perks up at that and pushes past me. "My father?"

"Yes, child," my dad drawls. "You haven't met him yet?"

Grace shakes her head. "I've never met either of my parents."

My dad gazes upon her sympathetically.

"Father," I warn.

He ignores me. "Why, your father is none other than Connor Doyle, the notorious head of the Irish mafia."

I see Grace's knees give out on her, and I'm there to catch her before she collapses to the floor. She's shaking her head. "No," she denies the charge.

My father nods his head. "Yes. Didn't you ever wonder why there was never any record of your parents whatsoever? It's because Doyle wanted to make sure that none of his enemies could ever find out about you and use you against him."

"Use me against him?" Grace's eyes cut to me accusingly. "Is that why you took me? Is that what you were planning?"

"No," I tell her vehemently, willing her to see the truth in my eyes. "I took you before I ever knew he was your father, Gracie, I swear. I took you because I wanted you. I love you, *tesoro*."

"Dios Mio," my father curses. "You've fallen in love with Doyle's daughter?" My father spits at me accusingly. "She's our ticket to finally having control over that Irish bastard."

I growl and turn to my father as I push Grace protectively behind me. "You're not going to touch a hair on her head," I growl at him.

He raises his eyebrows at me. "I'm your superior first and your father second," he warns me in a low voice.

I don't say anything. I just stare at him stoically. My message is clear though, because he firms his jawline, his eyes flicking back and forth between Grace and me.

"I wish there was another way, son. I really do, but you're going to have to relinquish her to me now."

"Over my dead body," I growl. I'm not sure if my father cares enough about me to not kill me for my insubordination, but I mean what I say. I'll die before I let him take Grace away from me.

I watch with dread as my father reaches into his breast pocket and pulls out his pistol. He lifts it in the air and aims it for me, and the only thought in my head is what's going to happen to Grace if he kills me.

"No!" Grace screams and pushes back from behind me, flinging herself in front of me. I snatch her as soon as she does and push her back behind me. "Grace! What the fuck is wrong with you?" I snarl at her angrily, expecting the bullet to come zipping through my chest at any moment, but it never does.

I turn back to my father and see him staring at us, slack-jawed. If I didn't know any better, I would say there were tears glinting in his eyes as he lowers his gun slowly. "She would give her life for you," he says with a touch of wonder in his voice, and I already know what he's thinking. He's thinking of how my mother died taking the bullet that was meant for him. That's the kind of love they had. My heart starts to hammer in my chest at the magnitude of what Grace's actions mean. She was willing to take a bullet that was meant for me. While I'm pissed as hell that she put herself in harm's way like that, there's only one reason a woman does that.

I spin around to face her and grab her shoulders, looking intently into her eyes, searching for the truth. "Why did you do that, Grace?"

Her pretty little cheeks flush, and she looks down, but I'm having none of that. I tilt her chin up, forcing her to meet my gaze.

"Is it because you love me, too?" She bites her lip and then nods, and my heart swells so big in my chest it feels like it's going to explode.

"Is it Grace?" I prompt her. "I need the words."

"I love you," she finally tells me breathlessly, with tears glinting in her eyes.

I forget all about my father being there as I pull her into my arms and kiss her deeply with all the love and passion and obsession I feel in my heart for her.

When we finally break apart, I remember my

father is still there. His gun is nowhere in sight, so he must have sheathed it. I wrap a protective arm around Grace's shoulder and pull her against my side. "Grace is my woman, and you won't take her from me. To hell with your vendetta. This woman is going to be my queen."

At Grace's little gasp, I squeeze her hand reassuringly. True, I didn't ask for her hand in marriage, but it's the next logical step. She *will* marry me. That's non-negotiable.

My father stares at us for a long moment before his mouth pulls into a wide grin and then breaks out into a full smile. He starts laughing and claps his hands together before he congratulates us. He slaps me on the shoulder, and says, "So be it, son. So be it. We'll find another way to get Doyle. Welcome to the family, *princesa*," he tells Grace before he starts walking toward the door.

"Call me later, Massimo," he orders me, "after you two have sorted everything out."

I couldn't be more shocked if the man shot me, but once the door shuts behind my father, I pull Grace back in my arms. She's still looking up at me with wide doe eyes. "Queen?" she questions.

"Marry me, *tesoro*."

"But—" she begins, but I rush to cut her off before

she can over-analyze it and talk herself out of how she feels.

"Do you love me?"

She nods her head. "Yes."

"And I love you," I remind her, dropping a kiss on her puffy pink lips. "Let me continue to take care of you. Let me keep you." I coax her.

"Do I have a choice?" she counters back, a bit of that fire flashing through.

I frown down at her. "Would you leave me if I gave you the option?"

She stares up at me for a long moment, and I feel my heart begin to crack. Her eyes finally soften and her shoulders slump as she shakes her head. "No, I want to stay with you, Massimo."

God, I'll never tire of hearing my name on her lips. I tighten my arms around her and go in for the kill. "Then be mine in every way. Take my name." I place my hand over her stomach. "We may already have the beginning of our new family in here," I remind her that we didn't use protection.

Her face flames at the reminder of how many times she let me come in her last night without ever once mentioning protection. I don't know if it just slipped her mind or if she subconsciously wants the same thing that I do. "Be mine, *tesoro*," I prompt her again, more sternly this time.

Grace looks into my eyes for a long moment before she finally relents. "Okay, Massimo."

I cover her lips with mine, kissing her deeply. When we finally break apart, she's gulping in breaths, and I'm running my hands over her face adoringly, and then I kiss her again because I can't help it. One taste of her will never be enough. My *tesoro*, my Gracie, my everything.

Epilogue

Three Years Later

Massimo

AS IT TURNS OUT, marrying Grace is all we needed to get Doyle under our thumb. Now he listens to us and is in the process of making restitution for all the chaos he caused my family. He's frequently reminded that the only reason he isn't dead is by the grace of Grace. She wanted to get to know her father, and surprisingly enough, the man truly does seem to have a soft spot for her, despite the fact that he was never there for her growing up.

I suppose I get it, though. He did what he thought he had to do to keep her safe, though he could have kept her safe anyway and still been a part of her life had he not been hell-bent on wreaking havoc on my father. But that's neither here nor there.

I look at my Gracie now. Her belly is swollen with our second child. She's the perfect mafia queen. My father stepped down and retired from his position, handing the reins over to me after my show of strength when I refused to give him Grace. He claims that's how he knew I was ready—when I had something to believe in and to stand up against him for. He'd have done the same thing for my mother.

Although I'm not sure my father is entirely supportive of my decision to keep Doyle alive and paying restitution, he follows my lead and bows to my power now. Just because he used to be the previous mafia king doesn't mean that he doesn't know his place in the new order. He defers to me in all matters, setting a good example for the rest of our organization. He knows the men are watching and that it's important for him to lead by example in our world. I am grateful to him for that.

I walk up behind Grace and wrap my arms around

her, pushing her hair to the side to drop a kiss along the nape of her neck.

She places her hands atop mine where they're spread across her pregnant belly and leans back into my embrace. Her sweet berry scent envelops me, and I can't help it. I inhale deeply. "I should make a perfume of you. We could bottle your scent and sell it. We'd make a killing," I tell her in between laving kisses along the creamy column of her throat. "But no," I growl as realization hits me. "I'd be too jealous of other men getting to smell your sweetness."

"Massimo," Grace moans my name, and I already know what she wants. I smile as I guide her hands to hold onto the rail of the white picket fence of our luxury country cottage. Once my wife told me that she'd dreamed of having her own little cottage out in the country, I made it happen.

Of course, there are some compromises involved in it. We are outside the city yet still close enough where I can get to work as needed, and our cottage isn't a tiny little one-bedroom affair like she had originally planned. In fact, "cottage" is probably a stretch for what it is. I made sure it was designed in classic cottage architectural style, but we've got several rooms within our estate and plenty of land to make sure no one can ever come build next to us. I got the white picket fence she never thought she'd have just to complete her dream.

Our two-year-old is down for nap time with her nanny watching her. At first, Grace balked at the idea of bringing in a nanny. She wants to spend every moment she can with our children. It's important to her since she grew up without parents for us to be very present in our children's lives, and that's okay with me because my wife and baby girl are my everything. Jade has her mother's green eyes and my dark hair—and a sassy little attitude to boot. She's going to be a heartbreaker when she gets older, and I'll probably go to jail for murdering any boy that looks at her.

I finally talked my stubborn wife into hiring a nanny so we could still have a bit of alone time.

I place my hand on my wife's rounded belly again. "How is our son doing?"

He hears me apparently and answers himself as I feel a kick in my wife's belly.

"As impatient as his father," she laughs.

"Impatient?" I say in mock outrage. "I don't think you give me enough credit. I held myself back from tasting your lips for weeks, *tesoro*. I stayed away from this beautiful little virgin cunt with more control than a better man. I think I'm a very patient man."

She snorts. "But once you did kiss me, it was like bam! We're getting married."

I tilt her head back to meet her eyes as I grin down at her. "What can I say? That pussy locked me down after one lick."

Her face colors, and my grin only widens. I love I can still make my wife blush like an innocent young virgin. "Now spread your pretty little legs and remind me of why I married you."

Grace immediately obeys, gasping whenever she feels my tongue licking her folds from behind. I spread her ass cheeks and grab a handful of her ass in both my hands, massaging her gently as I continue to drink from the nectar between her legs. I eat her out until her legs are shaking and my cock is dripping like a faucet that's been left on. She's so wet all it takes is one thrust to have me seated inside her.

She's still so tight it's all she can do to take the entire length and girth of me. She does beautifully, though, as always.

The muscles of her sweet cunt are gripping and sucking on me greedily as I saw myself in and out of her. I'm not ten pumps in before I feel my balls churning.

As always, our bodies are in tune, and my wife is right there with me. She splays her hand on top of mine that's gripping her hip and screams out my name as her pussy falls open all around me.

"Yes, *tesoro*." I feel my cock swell as I begin to pump my load deep into her.

"I love you, Massimo."

Grace's sweet voice telling me she loves me warms my heart. I cradle her in my arms with her back against my chest, my cock still inside her as we ride out the afterglow of our coupling.

"I love you too, Gracie, my treasure."

THE END

About the Author

USA Today bestselling author Emma Bray writes intense, steamy romances with possessive alpha males who'll stop at nothing to claim the women they want. Emma's instalove stories are filled with heat, passion, and happily ever afters.

Want more Emma Bray? Go to www.authoremma bray.com to get a free book!